There are three cats
in this book. They're
on the next page...

For Gwyn

First published 2014 by Walker Books Ltd,
87 Vauxhall Walk, London SE11 5HJ

2 4 6 8 10 9 7 5 3 1

Viviane Schwarz © 2014

This book has been typeset in Kingthings
Trypewriter and hand-lettered by Viviane Schwarz

Printed in Malaysia

British Library Cataloguing in Publication
Data:a catalogue record for this book is
available from the British Library

ISBN 978-1-4063-4561-2

www.walker.co.uk

WALKER BOOKS
AND SUBSIDIARIES
LONDON · BOSTON · SYDNEY · AUCKLAND

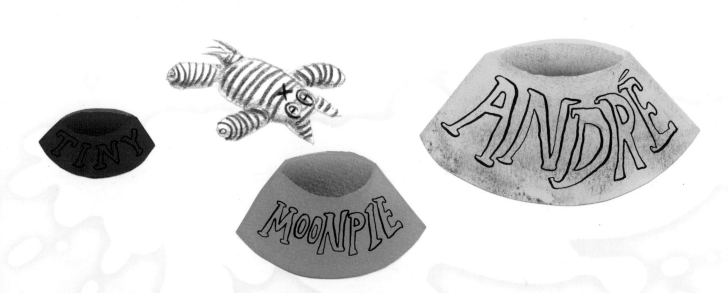

That piano was no good.
This wardrobe is much safer. Nobody open the doors this time!

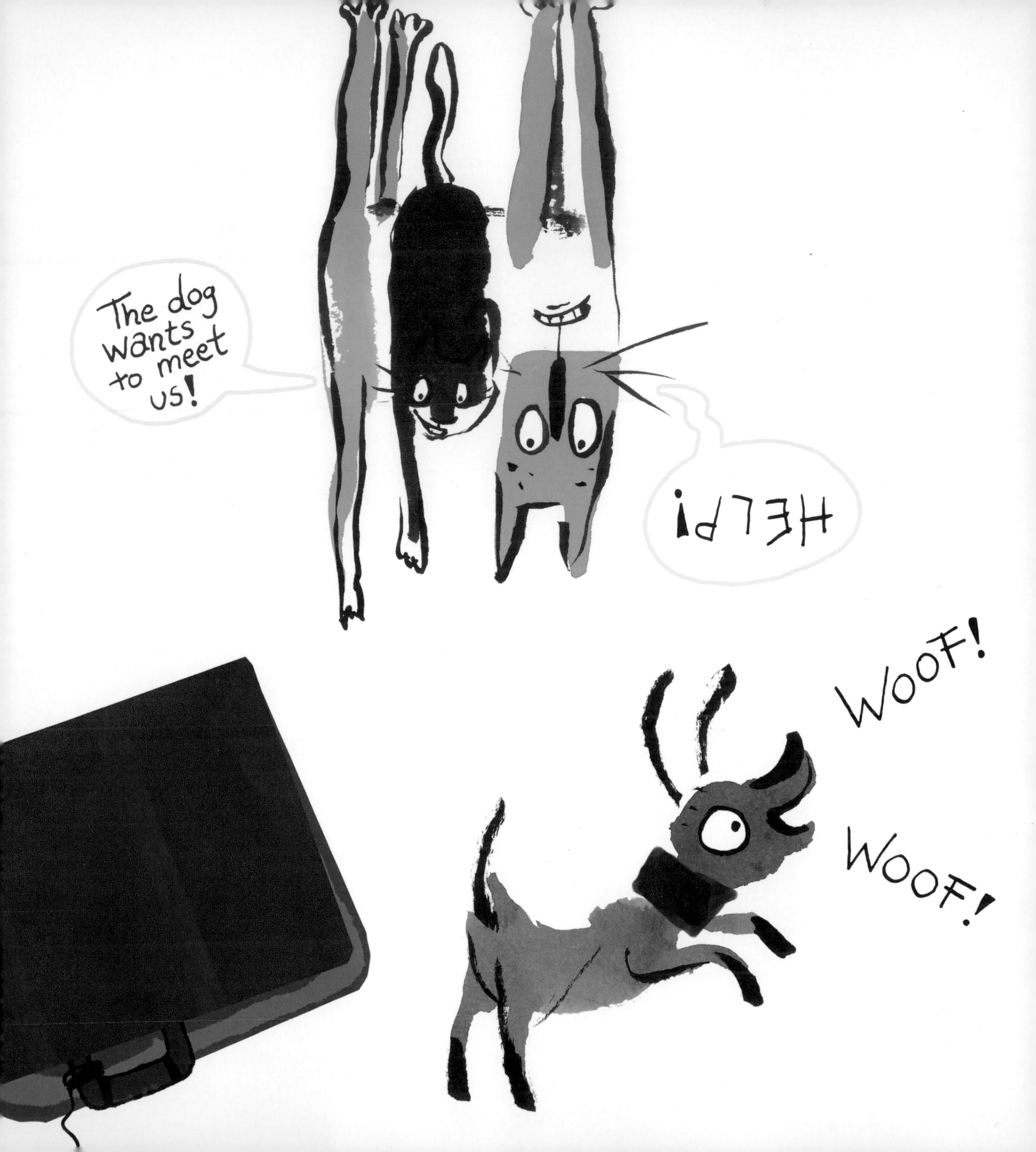
The dog wants to meet us!
HELP!
WOOF!
WOOF!

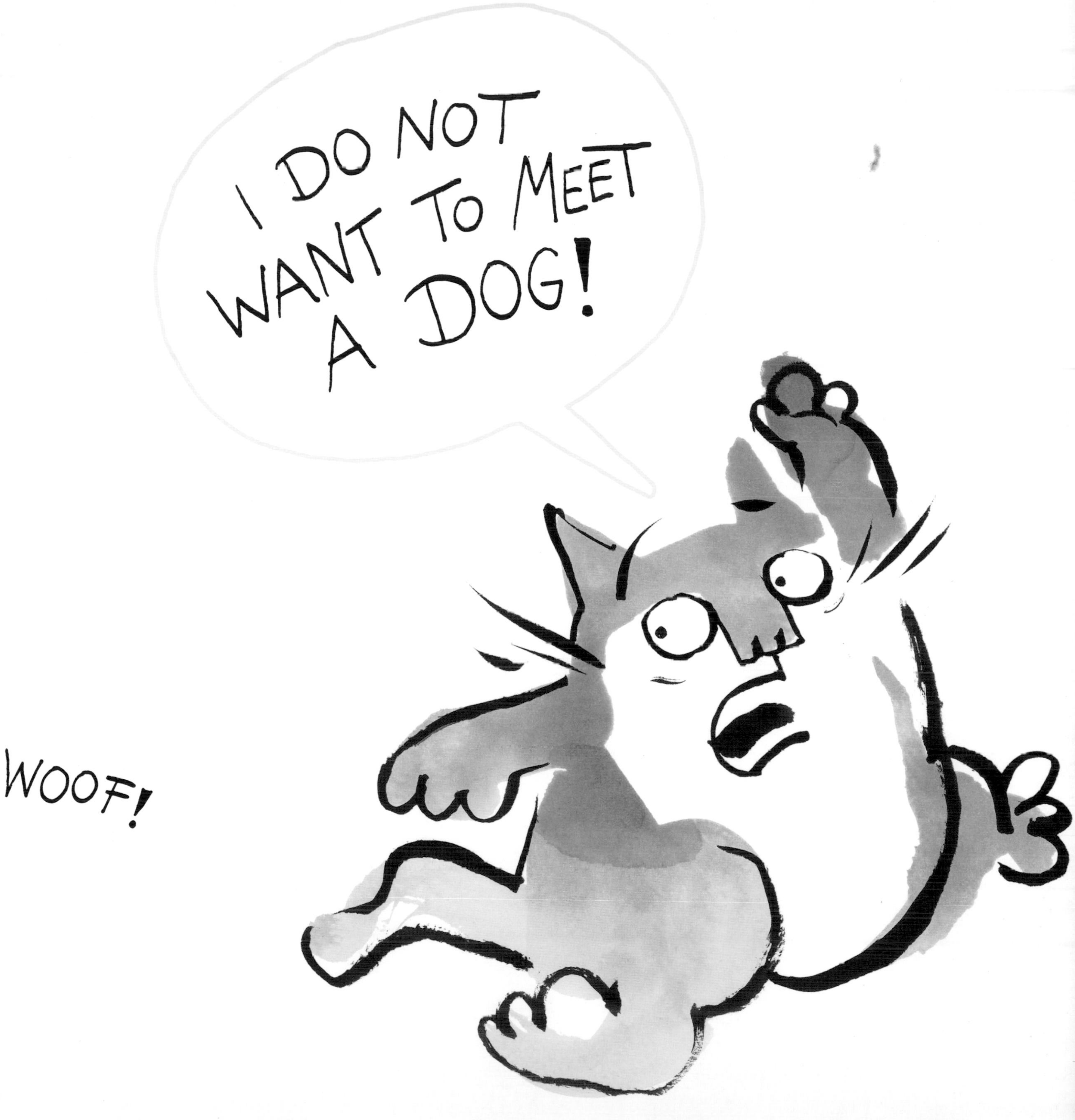
I DO NOT WANT TO MEET A DOG!
WOOF!

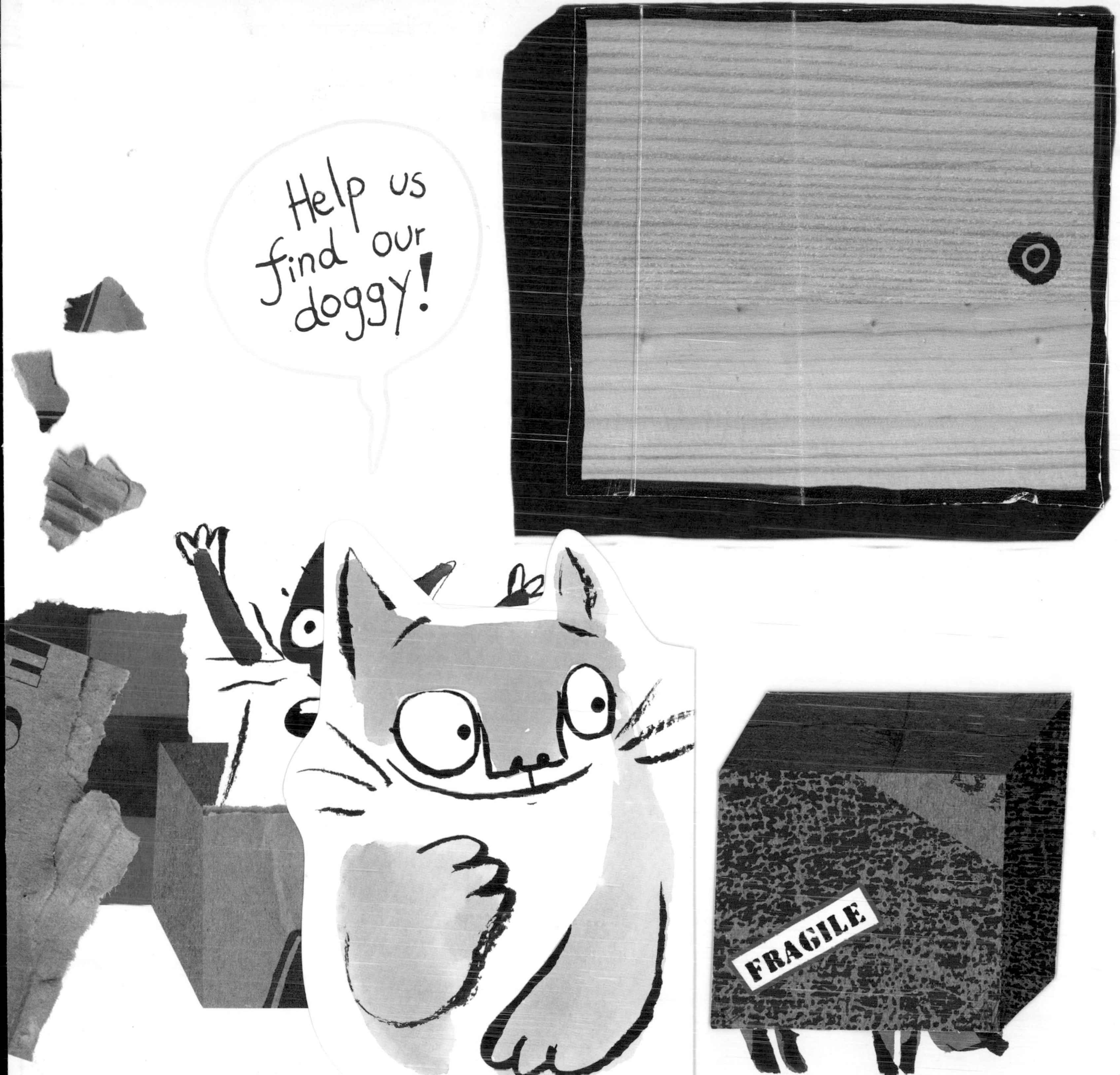
Help us find our doggy!
FRAGILE

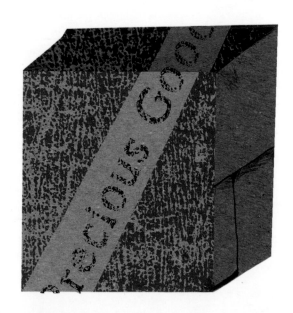

There are three cats
<u>and</u> a dog in this
book. They are all
your friends.